Meg the hen.

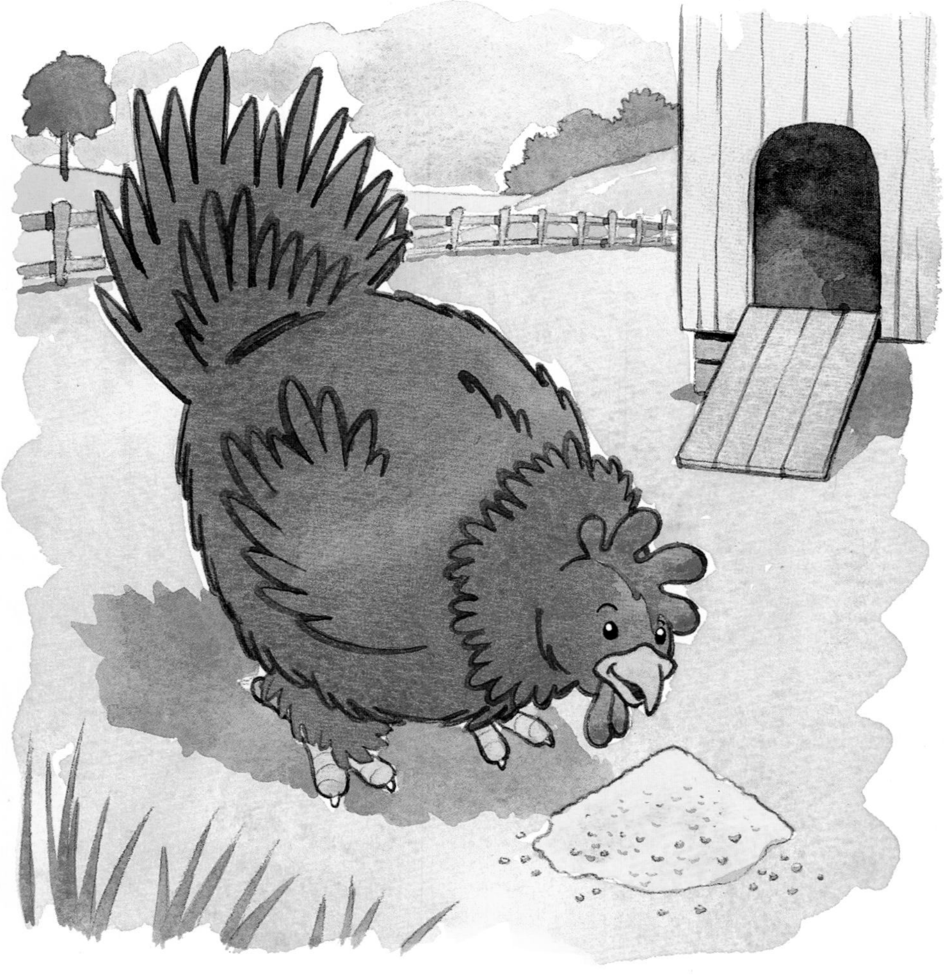

Meg is a red hen.

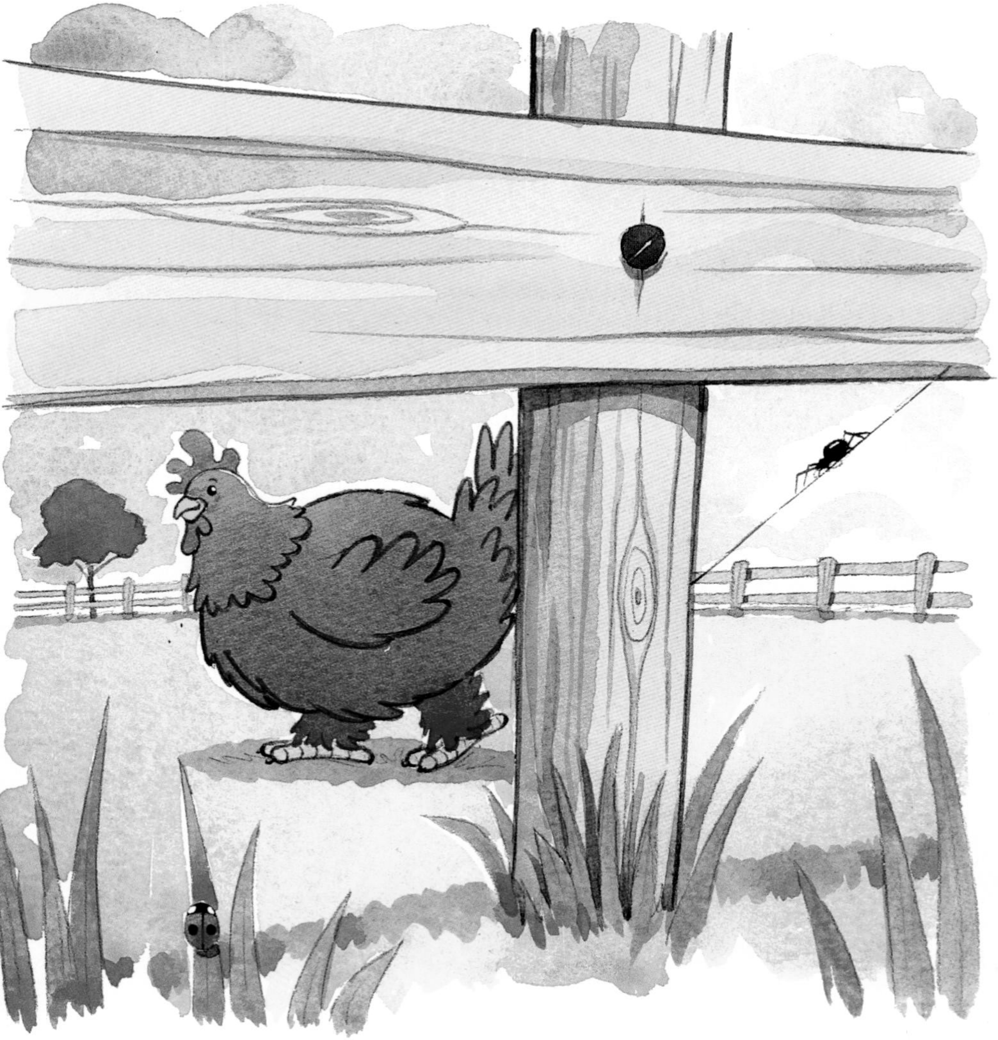

Meg is in a pen.

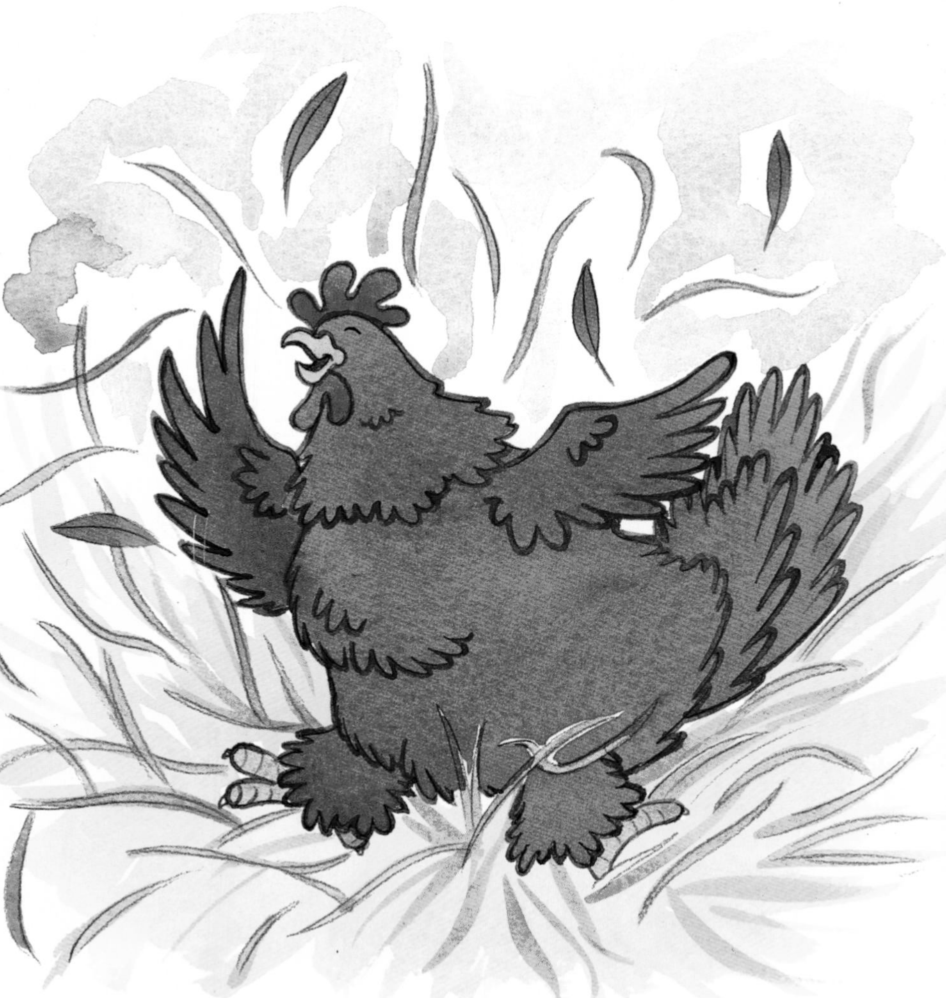

Meg the hen has fun.

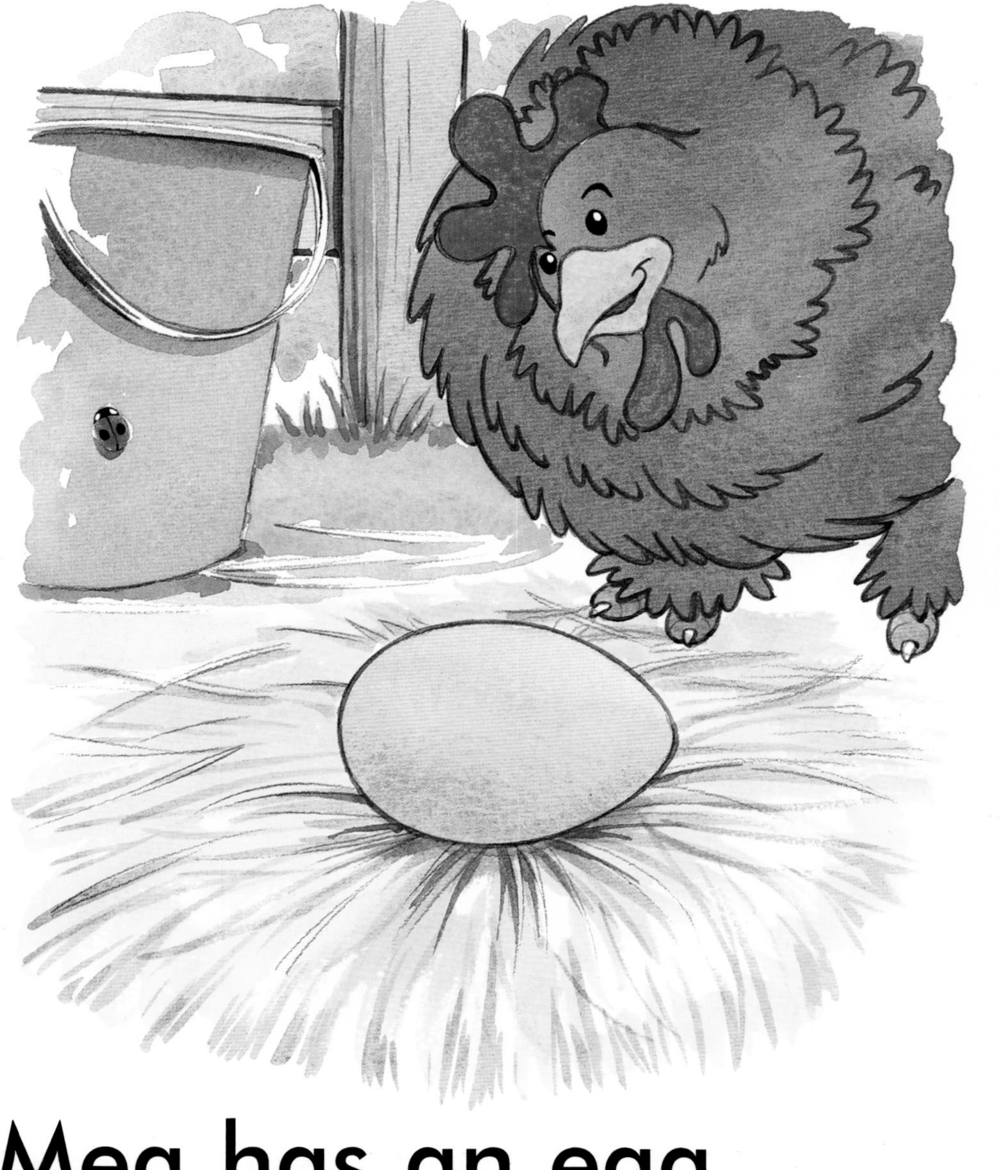

Meg has an egg.

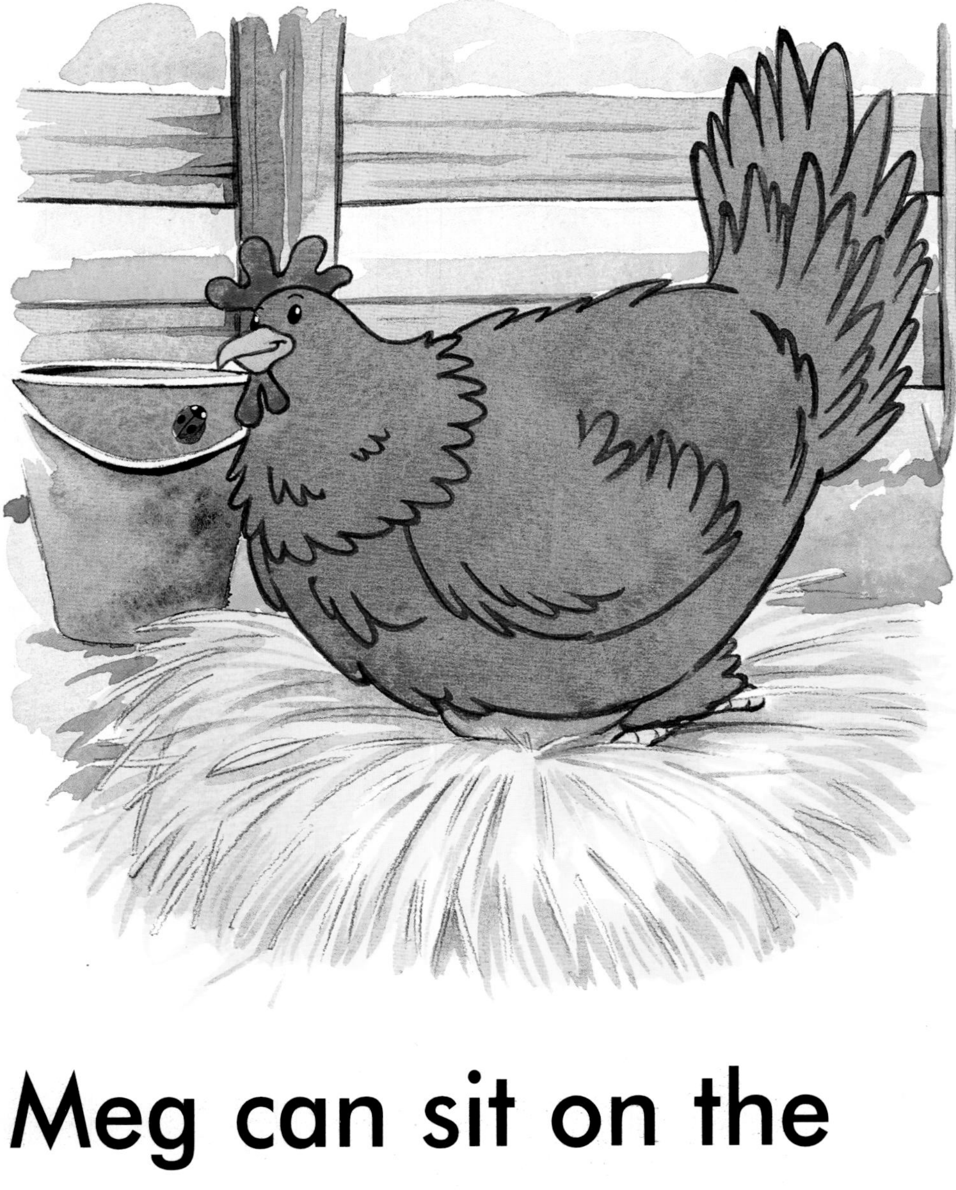

Meg can sit on the egg.

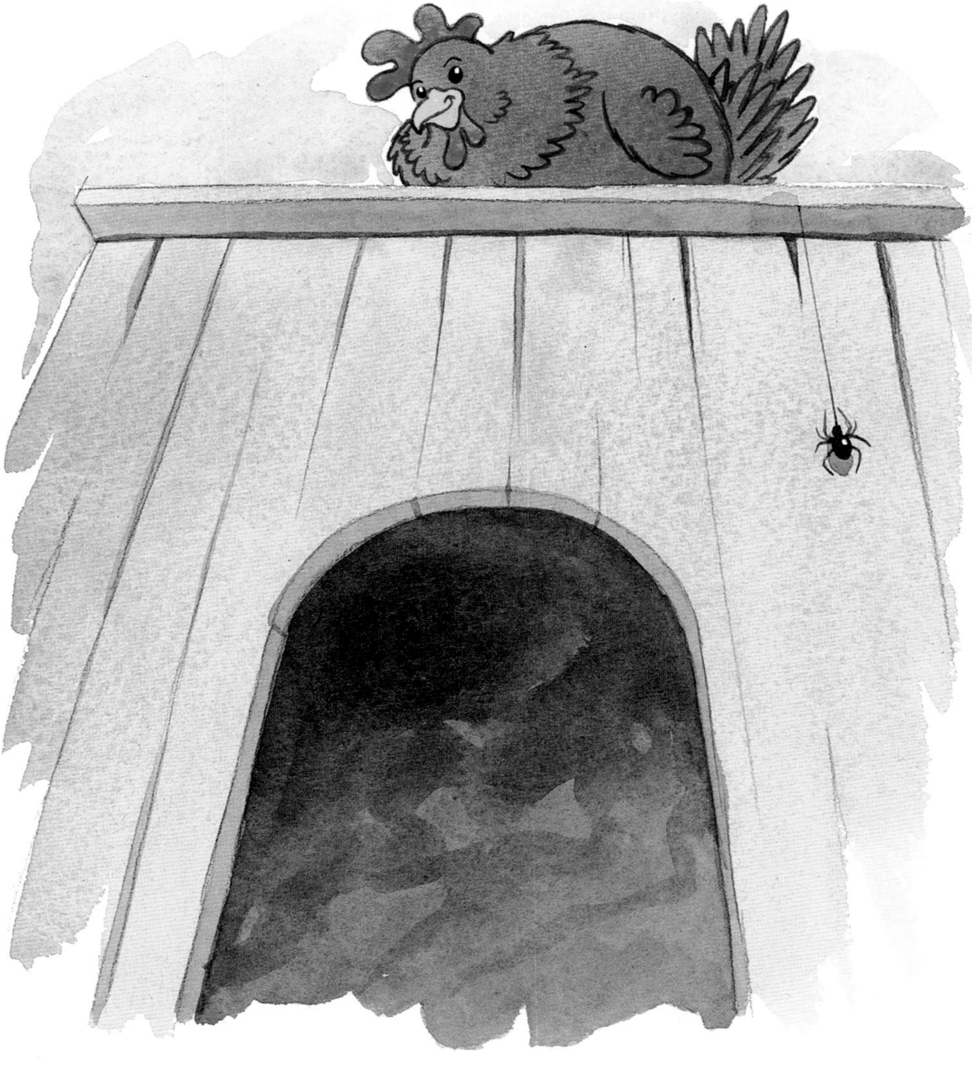

Meg is on top of the hut.

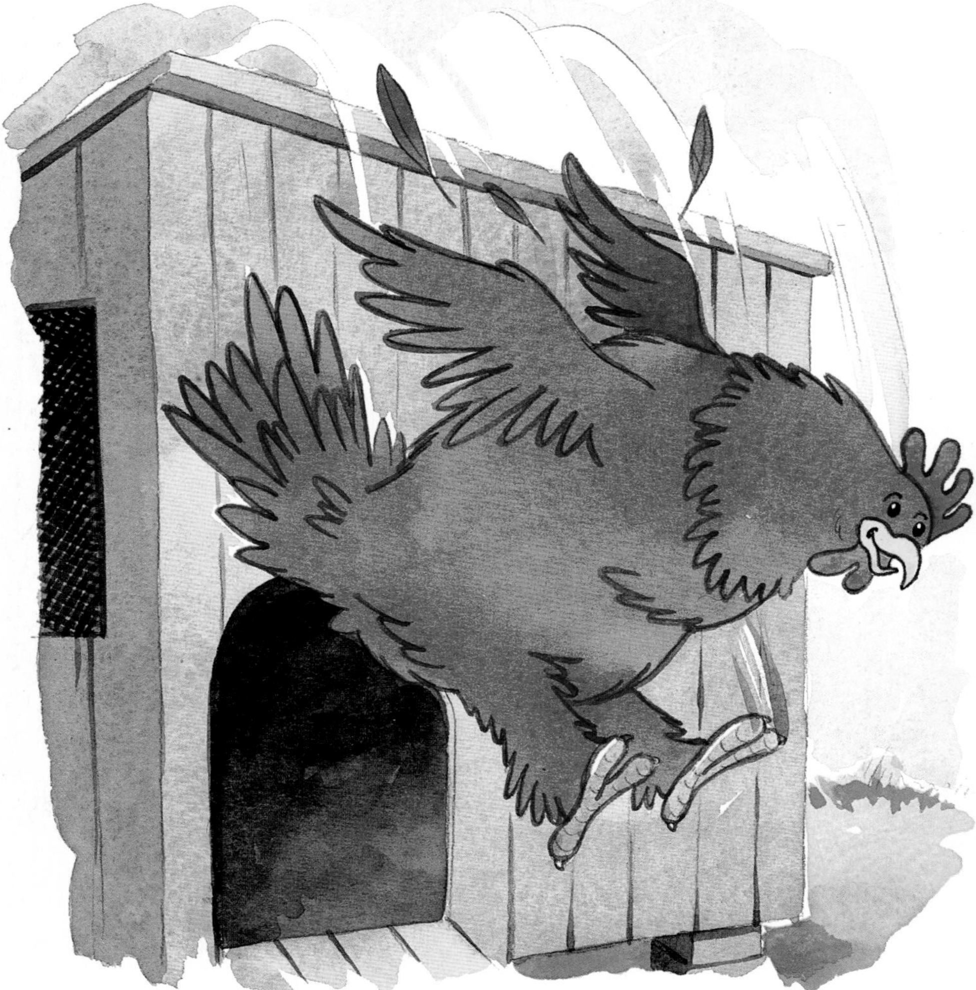

Meg can hop off the hut.